D0065960

THE MYSTERY OF
THE MISSING RED MITTEN

A PUFFIN PIED PIPER

THE MYSTERY OF
THE MISSING RED MITTEN

STORY AND PICTURES BY

Steven Kellogg

Library of Congress Catalog Card Number: 73-15439
First Pied Piper Printing 1977
Printed in Hong Kong by South China Printing Co.
E
12 14 16 18 20 19 17 15 13
A Pied Piper Book is a registered trademark of
Dial Books for Young Readers
® TM 1,163,686 and ® TM 1,054,312
THE MYSTERY OF THE MISSING RED MITTEN is published
in a hardcover edition by Dial Books for Young Readers
375 Hudson Street, New York, New York 10014.
ISBN 0-14-054671-5

FOR LAURIE

Oscar, I lost my other mitten. That makes five mittens this winter. I'm in big trouble.

I'll search every place I played this morning.

First I went sledding with Ralph.

Here's Ralph's boot, but there's no mitten.

Oscar, if you were a bloodhound, you could track down my mitten.

Look! Mouse tracks.

Do you think that the mouse and his family are using my mitten for a sleeping bag?

I'll look around the castles we built with
Herman and Ruth.

Here's Ralph's other boot and Herman's sweater and Ruth's sock. But no mitten.

Oscar! You found it!

Little bird, did you take my mitten?

Maybe a *hawk* did!

Do you think a hawk took my mitten to keep his baby's head warm?

I wonder if I dropped my mitten while I was making the snowman to surprise Miss Seltzer.

Hi, Miss Seltzer. Have you seen my mitten?
No, Annie, but why don't you look in the garden
where you were making snow angels?

I wonder what would happen if I planted this
other mitten.

Maybe in the spring a mitten tree would grow.

In the fall I'd pick the ripe mittens.

And on Christmas I'd give mittens to my family and my friends.

Oscar, my hands are getting cold.

Come on, Annie. I made some hot chocolate to
warm you up.

Miss Seltzer, the snowman is melting. What's that spot on his chest?

A snowman with a heart!

My mitten was the heart of the snowman!